Andi Far from Home

Circle C Stepping Stones

Circle C Stepping Stones #6

Andi Far from Home

Susan K. Marlow

Kregel
Publications

Printed in the United States of America
18 19 20 21 22 23 24 25 26 27 / 5 4 3 2 1

Contents

New Words

buenos días—Spanish for "good morning"

cable car—a type of transportation where railcars are pulled along a track by a heavy wire cable

chum—a close friend

contagious—describes something that is easily passed from one person to another, like illness or excitement

dandies—young men who give lots of attention to their clothes and appearance

despise—to strongly dislike; to look down on

epidemic—when a disease spreads quickly and many people are sick at the same time

parlor—a fancy sitting room used to entertain guests

physician—a doctor

quarantine—a time when sick people are kept separate from others so that illness doesn't spread

rig—a carriage with its horse or horses

scarlet fever—a disease with fever, a sore throat, and a red rash that was especially dangerous for children in the 1800s

spellbound—fascinated; very interested

stench—a strong, disgusting odor

waif—an abandoned or orphaned child who lives on the street

CHAPTER 1

Indian Camp

Spring 1878

"**H**urry, hurry!" Andi Carter bounced up and down on the wagon seat, where she sat between Mother and her big brother Mitch. "Can't we go any faster?"

"Only if we want to lose our load," Mitch said. "This isn't the smoothest road on the Circle C."

It sure wasn't. More like a cattle trail.

A sudden jolt sent Andi flying. She grabbed Mother's arm. "How much farther is it?"

"Not far," Mother answered.

Each spring Andi's family made a trip into the hills to visit the small Indian band that lived on their ranch. The Yokuts traded Andi's family for blankets and coffee and other goods. In exchange, the Carters took home baskets of nuts, smoked fish, and dried berries.

This year Andi had brought something special to trade. "Do you really think Choo-nook will swap one of her baskets for a doll?" she asked Mother.

A little bug of worry pinched Andi's thoughts. Choo-nook probably worked hours and hours on her finely woven, watertight baskets. Would she trade one for something Andi had simply bought?

Andi hadn't even earned her own money to buy the doll. She had used one of the gold nuggets she and Cory "found" at Looney Lou's a few weeks before. Andi's eyes had popped wide open when the shopkeeper dropped gold and silver coins in her hand as change.

That gold nugget was sure worth a lot of money!

Mother patted Andi's arm. "Of course Choo-nook will trade. She'll love the special clothes you made for the doll."

Andi brightened. She had spent hours sewing a little Yokut outfit. The stitches weren't perfect, but Melinda wasn't here to make fun of them. Her big sister was at school in far-off San Francisco.

Sitting still to sew is the same thing as sitting still to weave a basket, Andi thought with a smile.

Before long, she spotted smoke rising from a campfire. "There it is, Mitch." She pointed off in the distance.

Mitch clucked to Barney and Jingo. The matched pair of bay horses picked up their pace.

Andi held on to her seat with both hands. The wagon rattled over the bumpy ground. "I wish I was riding Taffy," she muttered.

Mother and Mitch looked like they wished they were riding horseback too.

Mitch finally pulled the wagon to a stop a little ways from half a dozen grass dwellings. Two barking dogs ran toward them. Other than that, the camp was strangely silent.

"Choo-nook!" Andi shouted. She climbed over Mitch and hopped off the wagon.

Choo-nook didn't answer. Neither did anybody else.

Andi looked around. The Yokut children usually ran and played in the camp. The women tended the fire, made acorn mush, or worked on their baskets.

Not today.

"Choo-nook! Where are you?" Andi called, using the few Yokut words she knew.

Just then Choo-nook's mother, Wa-see-it, stepped through the opening of their small home. She put a finger to her lips. "Shh. Choo-nook not well," she said in broken English.

Andi stopped short. Not well? "What's wrong with her?" She took a step toward the grass hut. "May I see her?"

Mother hurried over and grasped Andi's arm. "Not now, Andrea. It's best if you stay back until we learn more." She turned to Wa-see-it. "How long has your daughter been ill?"

Wa-see-it shook her head. She did not understand Mother's words.

Soon, other women appeared from their huts. One of the men came into camp from the direction of the river. He greeted Mother and Mitch but didn't smile. He handed Wa-see-it a basket of cool water.

The Yokut woman ducked back inside the hut.

"What's going on, Lum-pa?" Mother asked.

Lum-pa's English was excellent. "Choo-nook's throat burns like fire, and she is very hot. Her head hurts. Three other children are sick too." His dark eyes looked worried. "Can you help them?"

"We will do whatever we can," Mother said. "Mitch will fetch the doctor from town as soon as we return home."

She laid a hand on Lum-pa's arm. "It's not yet time to worry, but it would be good to pray. Let's hope this sickness is nothing serious."

Lum-pa nodded.

Without another word, Mother took Andi back to the wagon.

Andi let out a breath. They had come all this way, and now they had to turn back? On account of a fever and a sore throat?

"Can't I even say hello to Choo-nook?" she asked.

"Not today," Mother said.

Mitch was busy unloading the wagon. "You might as well keep the supplies," he told Lum-pa. "We can settle up later."

Andi grabbed the doll from the top of the pile and gave it to Lum-pa. "This is for Choo-nook. Maybe it will help her feel better."

Andi didn't care about getting a basket in return. Not now. Like Mitch said, they could trade later. It was more important for Choo-nook and the other children to get well.

Lum-pa smiled. "Thank you, little one."

Five minutes later, they were on their way home. Mitch kept the horses at a fast trot. The wagon lurched over rocks and past gopher hills. Mother bounced with the wagon but didn't say a word.

Andi gritted her teeth and held on.

The ranch house came into view in half the time it had taken them to ride up to the Yokut camp. Andi felt shaky when Mitch helped her down.

"I'll be back with Doc Weaver as soon as I can." He hurried inside the barn for his horse.

It was a long wait before Mitch returned. Mother paced back and forth and kept looking at the tall grandfather clock. It bonged two times. Then it bonged three times.

What's all the fuss about? Andi wondered.

14

Andi had been sick with a fever and sore throat plenty of times. Last winter her scratchy throat kept her home from school. A day later, a stuffy nose and a cough put her to bed.

But Dr. Weaver never came by to see her. Why was Mother in such a hurry to fetch him this time?

Andi was up in the hayloft playing with Bella's new kittens when Mitch returned. By the time she climbed down the ladder and peeked out the barn doors, Mother had changed clothes and was mounting her horse.

She and the men galloped out of the yard without saying good-bye.

The rest of the afternoon dragged. Andi trotted Taffy around the yard. She didn't ride up to her special spot, though. What if Mother and Dr. Weaver returned while Andi was away?

She led Taffy into her stall and brushed her. She combed out her cream-colored mane. Then she combed out her tail. It took a long time. Her stomach rumbled. It was getting close to suppertime.

A few minutes later, Andi heard hoofbeats. Mother! She poked her head out the barn doors to see if the riders had returned.

She sighed. It was only the ranch hands returning to the cookhouse after a hard day's work. Chad came home too, and Justin returned from his lawyer job in town.

Supper came and went.

Andi sat on the back steps with her chin propped in her hands. Just across the yard, the cowhands were relaxing on one of the bunkhouse porches. Diego strummed his guitar and sang a Spanish cowboy song.

At any other time, Andi would have joined the cowhands. This warm spring evening, though, she didn't feel like singing or listening to tall tales. Where was Mother? Where was Dr. Weaver?

With a lump in her throat, Andi said a prayer for Choo-nook.

The sun was setting when Mother and Mitch returned.

Andi jumped off the porch. "Where's Dr. Weaver? Is Choo-nook all right? What about the other children?"

"Give Mother a chance to breathe," Mitch broke in. He helped her down from the horse. "She's pretty tired. Doc Weaver headed back to town."

There were dark circles under Mother's eyes. She looked troubled.

Andi swallowed. "Is Choo-nook all right?"

"For now." Mother smiled and took Andi's hand. "Come along. It's getting late."

Chad and Justin met them inside.

"What's up?" Chad asked.

Mother took a deep breath and looked at her two oldest sons. "It's scarlet fever."

≍ CHAPTER 2 ≍

Scarlet Fever

Silence fell over the family. It felt like a dark, wet cloud had suddenly covered the sun.

Andi shivered, but she didn't know what was wrong. It was so still she could hear the *tick-tock* of the grandfather clock in the hallway.

Justin finally broke the silence. "Dr. Weaver is sure about this?"

Mother nodded.

"What's scarlet fever?" Andi asked. "Is it like the fever I had last winter?"

"No, sweetheart," Mother said. "It is much more serious. But it's nothing you need to worry about. Go on up to bed. I'll be there in a minute."

"But what *is* it?"

"Andrea."

Mother didn't say anything more. She didn't have to. Andi closed her mouth and turned toward the wide staircase.

No fair!

Like always, she was being sent to bed so the grown-ups could talk. Prickles crept up her neck. Something was terribly wrong.

Andi didn't hurry. She dragged her feet and strained her ears while her mother and brothers headed for the large sitting room.

"Dr. Weaver wasn't surprised to find scarlet fever at the Yokut camp," Mother was saying. "Just today he treated several unexpected cases in town. He wants the school closed right away to keep it from spreading."

Andi put one foot on the bottom step of the staircase. *No school? Yipp—*

"It popped up out of nowhere at the camp," Mother said. "Perhaps one of their people visited town and brought it back?"

Andi took two more steps so nobody could say she was not obeying.

"We don't know how scarlet fever spreads," Justin said. "But I'll ride into town first thing in the morning. Sunday or not, the school board had better meet. The doctor is right. We'll close school until this scare passes."

"It's a good start, but it might not be enough,"

Mother said. "I remember the last epidemic. It spread so fast." Her voice caught. "It's the children who are in danger, like little Choo-nook. They can't fight this fever. I . . . I'm afraid for your sister."

Mother's words brought Andi's feet to a complete stop. *Why is Mother afraid? Does she think I'll catch it?*

Andi could not go upstairs. Not now. Not even if Mother scolded her for not obeying fast enough. She jumped off the stairs and ran into the sitting room. "I feel fine, Mother. I won't catch the fever."

"Good grief, Andi," Chad growled. "Why can't you ever do what you're told?"

"Chad," Mother said softly. "Not now."

Andi sat down on the sofa and threw her arms around her mother.

Instead of scolding her, Mother held Andi close.

Andi relaxed. *She's not angry that I didn't go straight up to bed.*

"No worries about Andi, Mother," Mitch said cheerfully. "She's safe way out here on the ranch."

"I hope so," Mother whispered.

Justin reached out and ruffled Andi's hair. "Did you hear the news, honey? School will be closing for a while. You get a holiday."

Andi had heard, but Mother's worry about the fever had shoved this wonderful news into a corner of her mind. "A holiday? Really and truly?" She sat up with a smile.

Justin winked at her. "That's right."

Andi's thoughts rolled around inside her head like tumbleweeds. They chased away the last bit of fear that had been creeping up on her.

No school! Hurrah!

Scarlet fever suddenly didn't sound scary. Instead, it was Andi's ticket to ride Taffy and play every day. The wild flowers were in full bloom. The trout were practically jumping out of the creek begging to be caught.

"No school!" She grinned up at Mother.

Mother smiled back.

Andi remembered Bella's new litter. "I can play with the kittens every day." She smiled wider. "Wait until Sadie hears about this! She'll be so excited. We can fish and race and—"

"I'm sorry, sweetheart." Mother laid a quieting hand on Andi's shoulder. "You and Taffy will have to play by yourselves. If scarlet fever can attack the Yokut children up in the hills, it could easily find its way to the Hollisters. Nobody knows where or when this sickness will strike next."

"That's why we're closing school," Justin said. "It's called a quarantine. We want to keep you children away from each other so the fever doesn't spread."

Pop!

Andi's happy bubble burst. She slumped. Some of the brightness went out of her holiday plans. "Scarlet fever must be *very* dangerous if I can't even play with Sadie."

Mother nodded. "It is. If the fever gets out of hand, it could turn into an epidemic."

"What's that?"

"It's when so many children catch the disease that nobody can stop it," Mother explained. "Scarlet fever is very contagious. That's why I didn't let you go near Choo-nook today. I wasn't sure she had it, but I was afraid she might."

Andi grew quiet. Mother sounded worried again.

"It's also why I don't want you to go near Sadie, even if she seems fine." Mother paused, and her voice turned firm. "Do you understand me?"

"Yes, ma'am." Andi's heart thumped. "If I see Sadie hanging around my special spot, I'll turn around and gallop home as fast as I can."

Mother drew Andi into another hug. "I'm sorry if I frightened you, but children can die from scarlet fever."

Andi's eyes widened in horror. Die? No wonder Mother sounded afraid.

"Could Choo-nook die?" Andi asked. "Or Cory? Or my other friends at school? Or"—she swallowed— "or me?"

"Hey, now! Enough of that." Mitch pulled Andi away from Mother and swung her around and around.

When he set her down, Andi squealed. "Do it again!"

"You're getting too heavy for twirling."

"No, I'm not." Andi loved it when her brothers spun her around. "I don't weigh any more than those grain sacks you throw around."

Mitch laughed. "You got me there."

"Don't worry about your school chums," Justin said. "The quarantine will keep them safe, and you too."

Mitch's laughter had cleared away the gloom. Andi felt much better.

"Justin's right," Mother said. "Many parents will send their children out of the valley before this sickness gets too bad. The rest will stay quarantined."

"Which means no Sunday school tomorrow," Justin added. "We'll beat this thing. Dr. Weaver is running around like crazy to stop the fever in its tracks. Let's pray he is successful."

"Amen," Chad agreed.

Mother rose. "It's very late, Andrea. I'll take you upstairs to make sure you get into bed this time." Her smile showed Andi that she wasn't upset.

Andi lay awake a long time after Mother tucked her in and listened to her prayers. Part of her was sad and scared about Choo-nook and Cory and Sadie. The other part wriggled with delight at her unexpected holiday.

Worry and delight. Delight and worry. Up and down, just like a seesaw.

Delight won. *Oh, Taffy, what a fine time we'll have this week!*

Andi fell asleep wearing a smile.

⊰ CHAPTER 3 ⊱

Ranch Holiday

The sun shone warm and bright on Monday morning. Andi was up at dawn. Instead of her scratchy school dress, Andi pulled on a wrinkled shirt and her favorite pair of overalls.

She braided her hair and made her bed. Then she skipped down the hallway. Her hand slid across the banister railing. A quick slide would be the perfect way to start the day.

"Ay no, señorita."

Andi stopped short. *Oh, rats!*

She couldn't slide down the banister now. Not with Luisa standing at the bottom of the stairs waiting to scold her in Spanish.

Andi did not want to find herself on their housekeeper's grumpy side today. *"Buenos días,"* she said sweetly and hurried down the stairs.

25

Luisa looked at her in surprise. *"Buenos días."*

Andi brushed by Luisa and burst into the dining room. "Good morning!"

Justin's coffee cup stopped halfway to his mouth. He looked at the clock. "What are you doing up so early? We can hardly drag you out of bed on school days."

"It's not a school day," Andi reminded him. She sat down. "It's like every day is Saturday."

"Oh, I see." His blue eyes twinkled.

Andi ate every bit of her eggs and toast, swallowed her milk in four big gulps, and asked to be excused. "I have lots of chores to do."

Chad's eyebrows went up, but he didn't say a word.

Andi grinned. Usually her bossy brother had to remind her ten times a day to do her chores.

Not today. She had plans—big plans. Fishing was high on her list.

Andi rushed through her chores in the chicken pen. When two eggs broke, she called the ranch dogs. They cleaned up the mess in a hurry.

She slowed down after that.

When her chores were finished, Andi spent time grooming Taffy. "Those trout don't have a chance," she told her golden filly. "I'm going to—"

"Hey, Andi." Mitch poked his head into Taffy's stall. "Chad says if you want to help brand calves, grab your rope and come with me."

Andi jumped off the overturned bucket she used for a footstool and spun around. "I can help? For real?" Tingles raced clear to her fingers and toes.

"For real," Mitch said. "I'll saddle Taffy."

What a happy surprise! Instead of finding new ways to boss her, Chad was letting her help. But why?

The answer came quickly. *He's trying to keep my mind off this scarlet fever sickness.* She smiled. Chad could be really nice sometimes.

Andi found her lasso and plopped her hat on her head. She hopped from one foot to the other while she waited for Mitch to saddle her horse. "Hurry up before all the calves are branded!"

"Take it easy." Mitch laughed and handed Andi the reins. "It's an all-day job."

Andi followed Mitch out of the barn. She didn't go inside to ask Mother. If Chad had invited her to come along, then Mother already knew about it.

Mitch and Andi mounted at the same time. Their horses leaped into a lope before they left the yard.

"Wanna race to the big oak?" Andi asked.

Mitch barely finished saying "Sure!" before she nudged Taffy into a gallop.

They raced nose and nose. Andi begged Taffy to go faster, but she knew Mitch would win. His horse Chase was the fastest in the valley.

Taffy leaped ahead at the last second. The big oak tree looked like a green blur when she passed it.

Instead of boasting about coming in first, Andi frowned. "You let me win."

"Not me!" Mitch said. "But I can't speak for Chase. I think *he* let Taffy win."

Chase bobbed his head up and down. Andi laughed.

Half an hour later, Andi spied a temporary corral out on the range. It was a noisy, busy place. Dozens of bellowing cows and calves wandered around inside the large pen.

A small, hot fire burned at one end. Half a dozen cowhands were catching and branding the unhappy calves. They worked fast.

When Andi rode up, Chad grabbed Taffy's bridle. He squinted up at her. "You can brand any calf you can catch." He swung open the gate. "Go get one."

Andi lifted her lasso, chirruped to Taffy, and trotted inside the corral. Mitch followed along behind her, and the gate closed.

She looked around at the cattle. "This will be easy as pie," she told Mitch. "They have no place to run."

Andi and Taffy slowly made their way toward a group of cattle in the corner. The cows ignored the horse and rider until Andi dropped her lasso around a calf's neck and headed toward the fire.

The calf went wild. He bawled and twisted and leaped in the air. He yanked but couldn't get loose.

The rope was wrapped tightly around the saddle horn.

Mama cow mooed. The other cows scattered.

"Good job, Andi!" Chad called from the fence.

Three cowhands waved their hats and shouted, "Yee-haw!"

Andi beamed.

When she neared the branding fire, two cowhands flipped the squirming calf onto its side.

Thud! The calf landed in the dirt. He bawled louder, but Andi knew he wasn't hurt. He was just hollering for his mama.

Taffy stood still and kept the rope tight. She had learned her lessons well over the past year.

Andi patted her. "Good job." She slid from Taffy's back and ran over to the calf.

Mitch brought a red-hot iron from the fire and gave it to Andi. "Be careful," he warned. "Mother will skin me alive if you get burned."

He wrapped his arms around Andi from behind and steadied her hands on the long handle.

"I can do it myself," she said.

Mitch shook his head. "We're a team today, Sis. When you get a few calf brandings under your belt, *then* you can try it on your own."

"Besides"—Chad joined them to watch—"it's the only way Mother agreed to let you come."

The branding iron touched the calf's hide.

Smoke and a sizzling sound filled the air. The stench of burning hair made Andi's eyes water. She started to pull the iron away, but Mitch held it firmly against the calf's rump. He rocked it back and forth before lifting the iron off.

Roy loosened the rope, and the calf scampered back to its mama.

"He's not hurt a bit," Mitch said. "Calves have tough hides." He looked at Andi. "You have to hold that iron down for the full count, Sis. At least three seconds. Shall we try it again?"

"Oh, yes!"

The odor of too many cows in a small place tickled Andi's nose. She sneezed. Dust stung her eyes and scratched her throat. Sweat trickled down the back of her neck. By lunchtime she would be hot, thirsty, and covered in dirt.

But Andi wouldn't trade this morning for all the gold in California. She scrambled up on Taffy. It took less than a minute to get her rope ready for the next calf.

She spotted one right away. He had stepped away from his mama.

Andi's first throw landed neatly around the calf's neck. She dallied the rope around the saddle horn and started dragging the lively calf to the fire.

This calf was bigger and stronger. He put up a real fight.

31

"Did you see that, Mitch?" she asked when the cowhands had wrestled the kicking calf to the ground.

Mitch didn't answer. He was squatting near the fire, but he hadn't picked up a fresh branding iron. Roy sat next to Mitch with his head bowed. The cowhand looked tired.

Andi dismounted. "I'm ready, Mitch. Clay and Diego are holding the calf."

Mitch held up his hand and kept talking to Roy. Then he nodded, and the ranch hand rose to his feet. He looked wobbly.

Roy left the corral, mounted his horse, and rode away.

Chad hurried over. "You giving Roy the rest of the day off?"

"Not because I want to."

"Then *why*?" Chad snapped.

Andi winced. The ranch boss didn't like to be shorthanded.

"Roy's throat has been bothering him since yesterday," Mitch explained. "He tried to ignore it, but it's getting worse. I sent him back to the bunkhouse."

Mitch lowered his voice. "Roy was in town Friday night."

Chad shaded his eyes and watched Roy gallop away. "That's not good news."

A shiver went through Andi. Chad was right. It was not good news at all.

≈ CHAPTER 4 ≈

Epidemic!

The next three days were the best of Andi's life. She and Taffy played outdoors all day long.

She didn't see cowboy Roy. He was stuck in one of the bunkhouses under quarantine. The ranch cook looked after him.

"Poor Roy," Andi told Taffy on Friday morning. "I wouldn't want grumpy Cook taking care of *me*."

Taffy stamped an impatient foot. *Let's go*, she seemed to be saying.

Andi wanted to ride too, but she couldn't find anybody to saddle Taffy. She had just decided to ride bareback when the Circle C foreman stepped inside the barn.

Finally! "Could you please saddle Taffy for me?" she asked.

"Sure thing, Miss Andi." Sid dropped the heavy piece of tack on Taffy's back and left in a hurry.

"Thank you!" Andi called.

Sid waved and kept walking.

Andi cinched up the saddle and led her filly out of the barn.

She didn't get far.

"I want you to turn around and take Taffy back to her stall," Chad said when he saw her. "Then you go inside the house."

Andi stopped in her tracks. "Why?"

She got ready for a quarrel. Chad didn't like it when Andi asked why.

Too bad! Andi's chores were finished, and Mother said she could go riding. Her big brother could not stop her.

"Never mind." Chad grabbed Taffy's bridle. "I'll do it myself."

Andi stiffened. "Let go of my horse!"

Chad didn't yell. He didn't scold. He just looked at her.

"Listen, Andi," he said. "Two more cowhands from bunkhouse three are complaining of sore throats and dizziness. I sent them to bed. Mitch rode to town for the doctor. You need to stay in the house."

Chad's quiet voice scared Andi more than his bossy shouting. She gulped back her anger and dropped Taffy's reins. "All right."

Without another word, she turned around and went inside. Luisa fixed her a glass of iced lemonade and gave her two sugar cookies.

"Maybe Roy and the others don't have scarlet fever," Andi said. "It might be something else."

Luisa didn't answer. Her dark face looked worried. She sighed and left the kitchen.

Andi took her lemonade and cookies upstairs. She sat down on her bed. *Please don't let anybody else get sick*, she prayed.

Andi munched her cookies and read one of Mitch's dime novels. It was an exciting tale about pirates and sailing ships. She read clear to the end of the book—all sixty pages—in one sitting.

When Andi came out of her room an hour later, she heard voices. Dr. Weaver stood in the entry hall talking to Mother, Chad, and Mitch.

"I examined your sick men," he said. "Scarlet fever has broken out on the Circle C."

Mother gasped.

"The men are in no danger, Elizabeth. Adults don't even get the rash. But they'll feel pretty lousy for a week or two."

Andi sighed with relief. Roy and the others would be all right.

"A week or two?" Chad slapped his hat against his leg. "I thought this was a children's disease. How can strong, healthy men get sick? I need every hand."

"It *is* a children's disease," Dr. Weaver said. "But people of any age can come down with it. Even you, Chad. Or Mitch."

Chad snorted. "Not likely. I had it when I was a kid."

"You can get it more than once, so don't be reckless," the doctor said. "Stay away from the bunkhouse until this passes. Your ranch cook can tend the men. He knows what to do."

When Chad nodded, Dr. Weaver turned to Mother. "I don't want to alarm you, but even with the school closed the fever is still spreading. I'm treating over two dozen seriously ill children."

Mother gripped the doctor's arm. "What are you saying?"

"I thought the ranch would give you some protection. I was wrong. Folks are scared. They're sending their children out of town to friends and relatives in other parts of the valley. You should do the same for Andrea."

"Is it that bad?"

Dr. Weaver nodded. "It couldn't be much worse." He rubbed his forehead. "I'm about worn out from tending the sick."

"John—"

"I'll be fine." He gave Mother a tired smile. "I'm more worried about Andrea. Send her to Rebecca.

36

She'll be safe in San Francisco. I haven't heard of any outbreaks in the city."

"No!" Andi cried out from the top of the stairs.

Everybody looked up.

Dr. Weaver picked up his medical bag. "I'll take my leave. Do the safe thing, Elizabeth."

As soon as the door closed behind Dr. Weaver, Andi flew down the stairs. "Don't send me away, Mother. Let me stay here."

Her whole body shook. It didn't matter that big sister Melinda was in the city. Andi did not want to go to San Francisco.

Mother led Andi into the sitting room and sat her down on the sofa. "For goodness' sake, Andrea. Settle down. You've been to the city. We spent Christmas with Aunt Rebecca four years ago."

Andi remembered. Aunt Rebecca had bossed and fussed at her the entire week. Her house was so big that Andi got lost in it. Mitch had found her huddled in a corner in a spare bedroom on the third floor.

No, Andi did not have any happy memories from Aunt Rebecca's house.

"Please, Mother," she begged. "Don't send me to the city. I won't go near the cowhands. I'll stay in my room. Scarlet fever can't find me there."

"Shh." Mother laid a finger against Andi's lips.

"I promise you won't have to stay long. Just until the epidemic has passed."

"*How* long?"

"A few weeks. Maybe a month."

Andi shot up from the sofa. "A *month*? My birthday is in just a few weeks. Will I be home in time for that?"

Mother didn't answer.

"Mother, will I be home for—"

"We will hope for the best."

That meant no.

Andi slumped back on the sofa. She blinked back tears.

"Listen to me." Mother pulled Andi close and gently stroked her hair. "I want you away from this sickness. This is not the first time scarlet fever has struck the Circle C."

Andi sat up and rubbed her watery eyes.

"Chad and Justin were very young," Mother said. "Mitch was a baby. Father and I didn't send them away in time. The fever passed over Mitch, but the other boys came down with it."

Mother's eyes glistened with tears. "Your brothers were so sick. Chad just lay there. We"—she choked—"we almost lost him."

Fear curled around Andi's heart. Tall, strong Chad almost died when he was a little boy? From this same sickness?

Mother dabbed her eyes with a hankie. "I won't make the same mistake this time, sweetheart. I won't take the chance of you getting sick because I did not act quickly enough."

Her voice turned firm. "You will go to the city, and you will make the best of it. Is that clear?"

Andi looked up. Mother's face was pale. *She's really frightened.*

"Yes, Mother," Andi answered. "I'll go."

But she wouldn't like it. Not one little bit.

⇥ CHAPTER 5 ⇤

Off to the City

When Mother made up her mind to do something, she acted quickly. That same afternoon she sent everybody scurrying around like ants.

Mitch rode into town to telegraph Aunt Rebecca. Luisa scooted up to the attic and found a small trunk for Andi's clothes. Justin bought train tickets for the next day. Chad put Taffy out on the range.

Andi stayed out of the way. Her whole world had turned upside down, and she felt sick to her stomach.

A bright spot came just before supper.

Mother walked into Andi's room and said, "I'm taking you to the city myself, sweetheart. It will be a special trip, just the two of us."

Andi's belly stopped quivering. San Francisco

would not be so bad if Mother came along. Maybe she would stay a few days before going home.

Mother peeked inside Andi's trunk. She lifted a pair of overalls from the pile of clothes. "You won't need these." She pulled out a shirt and Andi's wide-brimmed hat. "Or these. San Francisco is not the Circle C."

Andi wrinkled her nose. Dresses—most likely scratchy ones—were waiting for her in the city. Aunt Rebecca loved to dress Andi up like a silly china doll.

Mother dug deeper. She held up two thin paperback books. "You had better leave these at home too. Your aunt despises dime novels. She'll throw them away. I don't think Mitch would like that, do you?"

Worse and worse. But Mother was right.

Andi put the books back on her shelf.

"Let's go down for supper," Mother said when Andi closed the trunk lid.

Nobody said much during the meal. Everybody looked too tired to talk, especially Mitch. He excused himself before dessert and went to bed.

Andi also went to bed early. She lay awake and thought about tomorrow's train ride. It would be the best part of the trip.

Railroad cars used to make her sick. Not anymore. She liked to press her nose against the window and watch the landscape speed by faster than a galloping horse.

She smiled in the dark and fell asleep.

A gentle shake woke Andi early the next morning. She yawned and sat up.

"Dress quickly," Mother said. "The train leaves in less than two hours."

"The early train?" Andi's eyes flew wide open. "I thought we were taking the noon train."

Mother hurried Andi out of bed. She pulled a petticoat and dress over Andi's head. Her fingers shook as she buttoned her up.

"What's wrong?" Andi asked.

"There's been a change of plans, sweetheart. Mitch got sick during the night. The fever is now in our home. We have to leave quickly."

Andi's heart skipped a beat. "Not Mitch too!"

"Don't worry," Mother calmed her. "He's miserable, not dying. He wants to go out to the bunkhouse with the rest of the sick men. I won't let him, but the minute I leave he'll—"

"You can't leave," Andi said in a rush. "You have to stay home with Mitch. Justin can take me to the city, can't he?"

She had wanted Mother to go with her, but not now. Not when Mitch was sick.

"He probably can," Mother agreed. "But are you sure?"

Andi nodded.

Riding the train with her oldest and favorite brother would be just as nice as riding with Mother. Nicer maybe. Justin would give Andi a dime to buy candy from the boy who walked up and down the aisle between the seats.

Mother hugged her. "I'm proud of you, sweetheart. You'll have a good time in the city."

"May I say good-bye to Mitch?"

"No, but he would be glad to know you're praying for him."

Right then and there, Andi and Mother prayed for Mitch. Andi added a prayer for Choo-nook and the children from town. Mother said one for Andi's stay in the city.

When they finished, Andi looked up. "Dr. Weaver said lots of people are sending their children out of town. Is Cory going?"

"No." Mother took Andi's hand and led her downstairs. "I didn't want to tell you, but Cory caught the fever."

"Cory's sick?" Andi gasped. "Oh no!"

Her whole world was falling apart. It was scary to know that a bad sickness was in the air. It was even scarier to wonder who might catch it next.

Maybe even me.

Andi swallowed. Did her throat feel scratchy? Did she have a fever? She looked at her arm. No rash. She wasn't dizzy, and her head didn't hurt.

She relaxed. *I feel fine.*

Justin was waiting for them at the breakfast table. He agreed right away to take Andi to the city. "We'll have a grand trip."

Andi could taste that candy already.

Mother hurried them through breakfast. She couldn't seem to get Andi out of the house fast enough. She talked fast too.

"Make sure you stop by Dr. Weaver's this morning before you leave," she told Justin. "I'd like him to take a look at Mitch. Another thing . . ."

On and on she went. Instructions for the train trip. Instructions for Aunt Rebecca.

Andi glanced up, puzzled. Mother looked ready to cry. "Mother, why are you—"

"We'd best be on our way," Justin said. He gave Andi a *be quiet* look and hustled her out of the dining room.

Mother followed them out the front door and to the buggy. She gave Andi a kiss and a tight hug before letting her climb onto the seat. "I love you," she whispered. "See you soon."

Andi swallowed the lump that was stuck in her throat. "I love you too."

Justin slapped the reins and they were on their way.

He spent the hour-long drive talking about all the interesting things Andi would see and do in the city.

She barely listened. She was too busy thinking about Cory . . . Choo-nook . . . the cowhands . . . and Mitch.

Dr. Weaver said grown-ups didn't die from scarlet fever. But what if this one time Mitch—

"Here we are." Justin broke into Andi's frightened thoughts. "I'll be just a minute." He pulled the horse to a stop in front of the doctor's house and stepped down from the buggy.

Justin didn't tell Andi to wait in the buggy, so she climbed down and followed him up the walkway.

Mrs. Weaver answered the door.

"Good morning," Justin greeted her. "I apologize for the early hour, but—"

"John's ill, Justin." Mrs. Weaver wrung her hands. "It's not the fever. He's too old and stubborn to catch what's going around. But he's worn himself out tending the sick."

She glanced at Andi and lowered her voice. "What will become of the children? If the doctor can't tend them, we might lose the little ones." She dabbed her eyes with a corner of her apron.

Andi heard every word of this bad news.

"It's terrible. Simply terrible," Mrs. Weaver whispered.

"I'm sorry to hear that, Lillian." Justin looked at Andi then said, "We'd best be on our way. Good-bye."

He led Andi down the porch steps. "I wish you'd stayed in the buggy."

Too late now.

Andi's insides swirled. "There's no doctor for Mitch? No doctor for the sick children? Who will take care of them if Dr. Weaver can't?"

Justin didn't answer. He pulled up to the train depot and began untying Andi's trunk.

Andi did not ask again.

They climbed aboard the railroad car. Andi plopped down on the red velvet seat and pressed her nose against the window. She blinked back tears.

Dr. Weaver is sick. Who will look at Mitch now? Who will take care of the children?

⇥ CHAPTER 6 ⇤

Too Many Rules

Andi didn't remember much about the long train ride. Or the candy. Or the ferryboat ride across San Francisco Bay.

Her thoughts were spinning too fast for her to enjoy the trip. No matter how hard she tried, Andi could not get Dr. Weaver out of her mind. He was the only doctor in Fresno.

What if the fever keeps spreading? she wondered over and over. *Who will take care of the children?*

Dr. Weaver always carried hard, smooth drops in his black bag. They soothed the scratchiest throat. He also had medicine that would help Mitch sleep. But what if he was too sick to bring medicine?

Andi was jerked from her daydreaming when the ferryboat bumped into the dock.

"Here we are! Welcome to San Francisco, honey." Justin smiled.

Andi looked around. Tall buildings reached high into the sky. Cable cars and horse-drawn streetcars ran up and down the busy avenues.

Bells clanged. Horses' hooves clip-clopped against the cobblestones. A ship's horn blew.

"It's huge," Andi exclaimed. "And noisy."

"That it is," Justin agreed.

A new thought cheered Andi up. A city this size surely had a lot of doctors, probably more than it needed. "Do you think we could find a doctor who would go to Fresno and help Dr. Weaver?"

"So that's why you've been so quiet all day." Justin smiled. "Let's get you settled before we think about doctors, all right?"

Andi nodded.

It didn't take long to hire a carriage. Justin gave the driver directions to Aunt Rebecca's mansion. She lived on a high hill. Andi could see almost the whole city from up here, and the water too.

Melinda was waiting on the porch. "Andi!" she shouted. "Justin!" She ran down the steps.

Andi flew into Melinda's arms. They hugged and jumped up and down until Aunt Rebecca scolded them.

"Land sakes, girls! None of that on the public street. Come indoors."

Andi looked at her sister in surprise. "I can't hug you when I want?"

"Get used to it," Melinda whispered in her ear. "Aunt Rebecca is full of city rules for young ladies."

I'm not a young lady, Andi wanted to say, but she pressed her lips together to keep the words from popping out. It was not a good idea to upset Aunt Rebecca.

The rest of the afternoon flew by so quickly that Andi forgot about her gloomy trip or her aunt's rules.

Melinda couldn't sit still. She didn't drink her tea. She wanted to hear all the news from home. Was anybody exercising Panda? What were her school chums up to? How were Chad and Mitch and Mother?

She cried when Justin told her about Mitch.

"He'll be fine." Andi tried to make her voice sound sure. "Dr. Weaver says grown-ups don't get very sick."

But a tingle of fear sneaked up her spine. *Will Mitch really be fine? Or Cory? Or Choo-nook?*

All too soon Justin stood up and said good-bye.

It was too late now to ask Justin about doctors. He had a train to catch. Perhaps Aunt Rebecca could help instead.

Andi and Melinda hugged Justin and waved to him from the front porch. "Good-bye! Good-bye!"

There was no going home. Not for a long, long time.

⚜ ⚜

Andi's first afternoon in the city had flown by, but the next day crawled slower than a muddy creek in summer.

Andi sat stiff and itchy in a church the size of a circus big top. When she twisted her neck to peer up at the high ceiling, Aunt Rebecca shook her head. When Andi wiggled or swung her feet, her aunt scolded her with a look.

It was the longest Sunday service of Andi's life.

Afterward, Andi curtsied and said "how do you do" to Aunt Rebecca's friends. She lost count after twenty-five polite greetings.

"You'll get used to it," Melinda told her.

Andi scowled. "No, I won't. Not if I live to be a hundred."

Melinda went back to school on Monday, but Andi was not as lucky. Aunt Rebecca could not wait to show off her little niece from the valley.

She helped Andi into a red dress with buttons, a wide collar, and a big bow. Before they left the house, she perched a floppy white hat on Andi's head.

"It is the height of children's fashion in London," Aunt Rebecca told her. "Ever since little Prince Albert wore his first sailor suit."

Andi made a face. Who cared what children in England wore?

But at least the silly outfit didn't make her itch. It was actually quite comfortable. She cheered up. Maybe a morning of calling on Aunt Rebecca's friends would not be too bad.

I will try my best to be a little lady, Andi promised herself.

She didn't budge an inch in Mrs. Roseburg's fancy parlor. She pressed her toes firmly against the floor to keep from sliding off the slippery cushions. Mrs. Roseburg and Aunt Rebecca talked and drank tea.

Andi nibbled a sweet cake and spoke when she was spoken to.

An hour later she ate a thin, crispy cookie in Mrs. Lansing's parlor. *I wish I was home riding Taffy.* But she did not speak her thoughts out loud.

Their last morning visit ended at the next-door neighbor's home. Andi perked up when she learned a little boy lived here.

"May I play with him?" she whispered when she and her aunt sat down.

Aunt Rebecca shook her head. "I'm afraid not. Brody spends his mornings with a tutor. Mrs. Stanton is strict about her son's education."

Andi slumped. Another hope dashed.

The morning calls wore Aunt Rebecca out. After lunch, she headed upstairs for a nap. "You may read or sew on your sampler," she told Andi. "That is how a proper young lady spends her afternoons."

I spend my afternoons riding Taffy. What would Aunt Rebecca say if she knew Andi had roped and branded calves last week? *She would probably faint.*

Andi bit back a giggle and followed the sour-faced housekeeper into the parlor.

"Sit still and don't get into any mischief," Mrs. Jacobs warned her. "And don't make any noise that might disturb your aunt."

Andi did not get into any mischief. She fell asleep. The only noise she made was a loud *thump* when she slipped off the sofa. She woke up in a hurry.

The long, quiet afternoons that whole first week gave Andi too much time to think. There was nothing else she was allowed to do.

No running, no skipping, no yelling or singing. No riding or fishing either. And most certainly no sliding down the banister.

By Friday she missed her mother, her brothers, and her filly so much that it gave her a headache to think about them.

Worse, Dr. Weaver might still be in bed. Andi had asked Aunt Rebecca more than once to help find a doctor who might go to Fresno.

"We will discuss it later," her aunt always said.

That meant never.

At least Melinda wouldn't have to go to school tomorrow. That was something to look forward to.

Andi looked at her sampler. It was a sorry mess.

Her stitches were as crooked as the man in the nursery rhyme who walked a crooked mile, bought a crooked cat, and lived in a crooked house.

She stuffed everything back in her sewing basket and stood up. Outside, the foggy San Francisco day had turned sunny. She could not sit still indoors one minute longer.

I wonder if Brody can play in the afternoons.

She would go next door and ask. All Mrs. Stanton could say was no.

Andi tiptoed out of the parlor and past Mrs. Jacobs, who was busy scolding the maid. She turned the knob on the front door. It opened without a creak. She glanced behind her shoulder for Mrs. Jacobs and took two steps—

She hit something large and soft.

"Andi!" Justin swallowed her up in a big hug. "You sure look pretty. Just like a little San Francisco lady."

"Justin!" Andi squealed. "Have you come to take me home?"

"Sorry, honey. It's just a quick visit. I have to catch the ten o'clock train back to Fresno tonight."

Andi's squealing brought the servants running to the door. Their scowls turned to smiles when they saw Justin.

Andi didn't care how much noise she made. Justin had come for a visit.

CHAPTER 7

A New Friend

"**I** had a court case in the city," Justin told the girls at supper. "Mother asked me to check on you and share news from home."

Andi was hungrier for news than she was for her meat pie and lemon custard.

"Mitch feels lousy, but Chad's fine," Justin said. "No more cowhands have come down with the fever. I don't know how Cory or Choo-nook are doing, but your friend Sarah is sick, Melinda."

"Oh no!"

"What about Dr. Weaver?" Andi held her breath. He had to be fine. He just had to be!

Justin looked worried. "Dr. Weaver tried to get up, but he fell over. Mrs. Weaver scolded him and put him back to bed."

Andi's heart sank.

Justin didn't stay long. He hugged his sisters and left at sunset to catch the ferry to Oakland. From there he would take the night train back to Fresno.

That night, Andi slipped into Melinda's room and crawled under the covers. It felt good to curl up next to her big sister after so many months apart.

"What's wrong?" Melinda asked.

"You heard Justin. Sarah is sick now, and Dr. Weaver can't help her." Andi sniffed. "He can't help anybody."

"The town council will take care of it," Melinda said. But she didn't sound very sure.

Andi was certain Justin would have told them if another doctor was helping out. "I have an idea." She paused.

"What is it?" Melinda asked.

"Well . . . I'm too young to ride the cable car or the streetcar by myself."

"That's for sure."

"But if you went with me," Andi said, "we could maybe find a doctor here in the city."

Melinda didn't say anything.

"Surely there is one kind doctor who would go help Dr. Weaver for a week or two," Andi said.

"I don't think finding a doctor would be the problem," Melinda said. "Aunt Rebecca won't approve of us riding the streetcar around San Francisco."

Andi learned at breakfast the next morning that Aunt Rebecca most definitely did *not* approve.

"Two young girls wandering the city alone? Knocking on doors like poor waifs?" She shook her head. "Absolutely not."

"Come with us, Auntie," Melinda boldly suggested. "We could ask your physician if he would go to Fresno."

What a perfect idea, Andi thought. *Hurrah for a smart and brave sister!*

Aunt Rebecca shook her head. "Dr. Wilcox is too old and too busy to leave the city and go off to the countryside. I wouldn't think of troubling him."

"Can't we at least ask him?" Andi asked. "You should let *him* decide."

"That will do, Andrea," Aunt Rebecca scolded in an icy voice. "Little girls do not tell their elders what they should or should not do."

Andi ducked her head and didn't answer.

"After breakfast you will go outdoors," Aunt Rebecca went on. "A little fresh air will calm your wits and help you to remember not to talk back to your elders."

"Yes, ma'am," Andi whispered. She choked down her breakfast. It was hard to swallow past the big lump in her throat.

The day did not get better.

Even though she didn't have to go to school,

Melinda did not want to go outside with Andi. She wanted to practice a new embroidery stitch she'd learned yesterday.

Embroidery? Andi made a face. *How dull.* She sighed and went outdoors.

She dragged her feet across the back porch and clomped down the five wide steps. Smooth rock walkways crisscrossed the large back yard. Andi followed the path that wound between colorful flower gardens and wide chunks of lawn.

"Good morning, miss." The gardener tipped his hat.

"Good morning." Clear across the yard, the carriage house stood, large and white. "Are there horses inside?" she asked.

"Yes, miss." He went back to trimming the roses.

Andi hurried to the carriage house and peeked through a window. One side of the building housed a buggy, a large carriage, and two white horses. The other half looked deserted and unkempt.

Whiz! An orange and brown blur darted between Andi's legs then vanished.

She jumped back, startled. What in the world was *that?* A squirrel? A chipmunk? Whatever it was, it had disappeared into the carriage house.

Andi dropped to her knees and crawled along the building's lower edge. Not far away she found a hand-sized crack between the boards. She pressed her face close to the opening.

It was too dim inside to see anything. She stood up and brushed the dirt from her dress.

"Hey there!"

Andi whirled at the voice. A little boy with red hair was peeking over the short brick wall that separated Aunt Rebecca's yard from the neighbor's yard.

He climbed over the top, dropped to the ground, and ran over to Andi. "I'm Brody Stanton. Are you Melinda's sister?"

She nodded. "I'm Andi."

"Nice to meet you," Brody said. "Have you seen my cat?"

The orange and brown blur! Andi pointed to the carriage house. "It ran inside."

"Cleopatra is *always* escaping." Brody let out a big breath. "I don't know why she likes your aunt's yard so much. I have to climb over and look for her most days."

"It's the mice," Andi said. "She went through a big crack in the carriage house to hunt."

"Really?" Brody's eyes opened wide. "Mama better not find out. She won't let Cleo back inside the house if she finds out she eats dirty old mice."

Andi laughed. "What else would a cat eat?"

Pictures of Bella and Mouser and the other Circle C barn cats flashed through Andi's mind. Without them, the ranch would be overrun with pesky mice.

"Cleo eats special food," Brody said. "She's a *house* cat, not a barn cat."

Andi laughed louder. "She looks like a sneaky barn cat to me. Come on. I'll help you find her."

She opened the door to the carriage house. The horses whickered a welcome, but Andi turned aside. She led Brody into the deserted part of the building. "I bet there's lots of mice in here."

They spent the next ten minutes peeking under dusty shelves and exploring corners thick with cobwebs. Andi climbed a ladder and searched the loft. It was empty. She hopped down.

"Cleo!" Brody called.

Just then Cleopatra ran past them carrying a plump mouse.

"There she is!" Brody lunged for the cat but missed. He tripped and fell.

Andi snatched the cat up. She growled, low and deep, but Andi held her tight. The mouse dangled from Cleo's mouth.

Brody gaped at Andi. "How did you do that?"

"Lots of practice." Andi yanked the dead mouse away and threw it in a corner. "There. Now your mother will never know what Cleo's been up to."

Cleo's golden eyes followed the mouse, but she didn't try to escape from Andi's arms. Instead, she nosed Andi and began to purr.

Andi stroked her. "She's a beautiful cat."

Brody beamed. "She's smart too. I'll take Cleo home, then maybe"—he looked wistfully at Andi—"we could play together."

"Sure! We can explore the yard and the carriage house, climb trees, and brush the horses." She passed the cat to her new friend. "Hurry back."

Brody left, but he returned five minutes later. A smile covered his freckled face. "What should we do first?"

"Want to climb an apple tree?" Three grew in Aunt Rebecca's yard. They all looked perfect for climbing.

Brody was only a little younger than Andi, but he had never climbed a tree. "I don't have the right kind of trees in my yard," he explained.

"There's nothing to it." Andi let Brody climb up first. He scrambled to the top and grinned down at her.

It was a wonderful morning. Playing with Brody was just as much fun as playing with Sadie or Cory. Andi forgot about missing the ranch. For a little while, she even forgot about finding a doctor to help her sick friends.

When Andi said good-bye and skipped into the house for lunch, her heart was overflowing with happiness.

Maybe San Francisco is not such a bad place after all.

⇥ CHAPTER 8 ⇤

Sunday Outing

"**A**ndrea Rose Carter!"

Aunt Rebecca's scolding voice stopped Andi in her tracks. Her happy heart dropped to her stomach like a rock. "What's wrong?"

"What's *wrong?* Your hair is a disgrace, your hands and face are scratched and filthy, and"—she peered closer—"are those grass stains on your dress?" She clucked her tongue. "What have you been up to all morning?"

"Playing in the back yard with Brody. We found his cat and climbed the apple tree—"

"Shame on you!" Aunt Rebecca sucked in a sharp breath. "Young ladies do not climb trees or soil their clothes."

The scolding stung. "I climb trees all the time on the ranch."

"You are *not* on the ranch," Aunt Rebecca reminded her. "Now march upstairs this instant. Change your clothes and wash up for lunch."

Andi's delightful morning went *poof!* She choked back a sob and ran up the stairs to her room. She fell across the bed and wept. Salty tears stung her cheeks.

Melinda came in and sat down beside her.

"Aunt Rebecca is mean," Andi sobbed. "All she ever does is scold. I want Mother. I want to go home."

Melinda tried to comfort her. "Don't carry on so, Andi. Aunt Rebecca's tongue is sharp, but she doesn't mean half of what she says. Come down and eat."

"I'm not hungry. Go away."

Andi cried herself to sleep.

Much later that afternoon, a gentle hand shook Andi awake. She rolled over.

Aunt Rebecca stood over her.

Andi held her breath. What had she done wrong now?

"It has been a long and difficult week for both of us, Andrea," Aunt Rebecca said softly. "You are worried about your family and friends and"—she sighed—"I scolded you rather harshly. I apologize. I've planned an outing for tomorrow afternoon. Would you like to come along?"

An outing? Andi sat up and rubbed the sleep out of her eyes. "Where?"

Aunt Rebecca gave Andi a rare smile. "It's a surprise."

⊰ ⊱

After church the next day, Aunt Rebecca shooed the girls upstairs. "Change into something comfortable," she said. "It's unusually warm this afternoon."

Andi was yanking off her scratchy Sunday outfit when Melinda ran into her room half dressed. "Take a look outside!"

Andi pressed her nose against the windowpane and squealed.

Aunt Rebecca's coachman had brought the carriage around to the front of the house. Two white horses pranced and tossed their heads. They looked happy to be out and about.

"We're going somewhere in style," Melinda said. "Maybe Golden Gate Park." She hurried off to finish dressing. "Don't forget your hat," she called over her shoulder.

Andi didn't know what Golden Gate Park was, but a carriage ride sounded mighty fine. Maybe Thomas would let her drive the horses. She buttoned up her red dress, grabbed a sun hat, and ran downstairs.

Thomas helped the ladies into the carriage, and off they went.

Clip-clop, clip-clop. The horses trotted along a

street choked with Sunday afternoon traffic. Buggies, carriages, coaches, and people on horseback jostled to find a place in line.

Andi wriggled with excitement. "May I sit up with Thomas?" she asked.

"Certainly not." Aunt Rebecca's face showed that she did not approve of little girls wiggling and wanting to drive the horses. "I expect you to sit like a little lady and enjoy the scenery."

Andi slumped. Maybe this outing would not be very pleasant after all.

When Aunt Rebecca opened a wicker basket and passed out sandwiches and thick slices of cheese, Andi cheered up. The cook had also packed cookies and a jar of cold lemonade.

Andi forgot about wanting to ride up top with the driver.

"Are we going to the park?" Melinda asked between dainty bites of her sandwich.

Aunt Rebecca shook her head. "You'll see."

The road went on and on. Soon the houses and other city buildings lay far behind.

The sun beat down on the open carriage. Not a breath of air cooled Andi's face. Sweat pooled under her collar.

"Can't these horses go any faster?" Andi asked.

A fast trot would stir up a breeze. A small one, but it would be better than nothing.

"Proper ladies do not race their carriages," Aunt Rebecca said. "This is a leisurely ride." She opened her parasol to shade her head.

When Melinda opened her parasol too, Andi rolled her eyes. Then she sat up. "Look!"

Several yards away, half a dozen horses were galloping toward them from the direction of the city. They kicked up dust on a wide dirt track next to the roadway.

"Yee-haw!" The riders shouted and urged their mounts faster.

"It's a race!" Andi forgot about sitting still. She bounced up and down in her seat and pointed. "I'm cheering for that bay horse. Oh, he's fast!"

She leaned over the side of the carriage and waved. Her heart was thumping as fast as the galloping horses. "Go, you beauty! You can do it!"

The bay's rider touched two fingers to the brim of his short, brown hat and pulled ahead.

"They don't look anything like the cowboys racing on the ranch, do they?" Melinda said. "More like slicked-up young dandies."

The riders did look overdressed in their long jackets, tight pants, and knee-high black boots. Their horses were sleek and long-legged.

Andi didn't care what the riders were wearing. "They sure can ride!"

"It's because they're using lightweight English saddles," Melinda said in her fifteen-year-old voice.

Andi didn't have time to ask her sister where she'd learned that. Another group of young men thundered by. They hollered just as loudly as the first set of riders.

Andi grinned. "What a good time they're having!"

When a third bunch of wild young riders flew past, Aunt Rebecca put a stop to Andi's cheering. "For goodness' sake, Andrea. Don't make a scene. Sit down and behave."

Andi obeyed. She shaded her eyes and tried to keep track of the riders.

It was no use. The dust hid them.

"Rowdies!" Aunt Rebecca huffed her disapproval. "Have they nothing better to do than disrupt a perfectly good Sunday afternoon carriage ride?"

When more horses and riders raced by, Andi cheered, but only on the inside. *I wish Taffy and I were racing.* She kept it to herself. Aunt Rebecca would not approve of Andi's wish.

Andi knew her directions. With the sun high overhead, she figured the riders were headed west. What was west of the city? "How far does the track go?" she asked. "Where are they headed?"

"Lands End," Aunt Rebecca replied. "That is also where this road goes."

Andi craned her neck to peek around Thomas and the horses. All she could see was sky and land and dozens of other rigs headed in the same direction.

"Is Lands End a park?" Melinda asked. She looked as puzzled as Andi.

"Indeed not," Aunt Rebecca answered. "There is nothing but the Pacific Ocean beyond Lands End."

Andi's stomach turned over. She had seen plenty of water last week, when she and Justin crossed San Francisco Bay. It looked cold and deep, but she could see land all around.

The Pacific Ocean? Andi did not want to go anywhere near that much water.

Aunt Rebecca gave the girls a pleased smile. "This is my surprise."

Andi gulped. *More like a bad dream.* "Have you ever seen the ocean?" she asked Melinda.

Melinda shook her head.

Andi reached out and grasped her sister's hand. At least they were in this scary adventure together.

⊰ CHAPTER 9 ⊱

Lands End

Thomas eased the carriage to a stop in front of a large, white building. An American flag stuck up high from the red roof. It flapped in the ocean breeze.

A sign just above the roof's edge read **CLIFF HOUSE**.

People strolled along the wide driveway in front of the building. Men wore tall hats. The women carried parasols. Children of all ages ran back and forth.

Everybody was dressed in their Sunday best.

Thomas helped Aunt Rebecca from the carriage. He gave Melinda and Andi a hand down. Then he climbed back into the driver's seat and pulled away.

Andi didn't know where Thomas would tie up such a big rig. Every spot along the long hitching rail in the horse shed looked taken.

Lands End was certainly a popular place!

The hard-packed road ran in front of the Cliff House. It also stretched down, away from the building. But . . . down to where?

Andi couldn't wait to find out. The Cliff House blocked her view, so she hurried past it. A long, wooden railing ran alongside the sloping road. She leaned over it and—

"Yikes!" Andi sprang backward. Her heart slammed against the inside of her chest.

Not even the tallest tree on the ranch stood this far above the ground. Her head spun, and she felt dizzy. She took two more steps away from the railing.

"Do be careful, Andrea," Aunt Rebecca warned. "It is a long way down."

"No wonder they call it the Cliff House," Melinda said in a hushed voice.

Andi couldn't speak. The building she had just run past rested on the edge of a high cliff. It overlooked the water. Just beyond the building, three enormous rocks poked up from the ocean.

Beyond the rocks lay nothing but water.

Curiosity pushed Andi's fear into a corner of her mind. She returned to the fence and gripped the top railing.

The sea breeze smelled like salt. It ruffled her hair and tugged at her wide-brimmed straw hat. She squinted against the sun sparkling on the water.

"What are those things moving around on those giant rocks?" She pointed.

Melinda came and stood beside her. "I have no idea." She turned to Aunt Rebecca. "Do you know, Auntie?"

"Those are sea lions. They climb up and sunbathe on Seal Rocks."

Sea lions!

Andi's mouth dropped open. She'd seen sea lions last summer when the circus came to town. Two of them had swum around in a small tank filled with water.

But here sea lions were everywhere. Hundreds of them. "Oh my!"

Aunt Rebecca adjusted her parasol and began walking down the long road to the beach. "Come along, girls."

Buggies passed them on their way down to the seashore. So did running, laughing boys and young men on horseback.

Andi wanted to run and skip, but she stayed close to Aunt Rebecca. No sense getting scolded. Instead, she imagined what fun it would be to ride Taffy along the beach.

Aunt Rebecca led the girls to a sandy place between two huge pieces of driftwood. "I know this place very well." She sat down on a log. "This spot is my favorite."

"Really?" Melinda said.

"Oh, yes," she replied. "Your father came to the city many times to visit your mother before they were married. The three of us often spent an afternoon at Lands End."

Andi and Melinda looked at each other in surprise.

"The tide is out," Aunt Rebecca was saying. "You might find sea creatures in some of the rocky pools. Since you have never waded in the ocean before, you may remove your shoes and stockings."

"May I"—Andi hardly dared ask—"run and play?"

Aunt Rebecca nodded. "This once. It is a special day."

Andi plopped down and tore off her high-buttoned shoes. She peeled away her long, hot stockings. Then she wiggled her toes in the warm sand.

How good it felt!

Melinda did the same, and then headed for the water. "Let's go wading."

Andi held back. She liked the warm sand, but the ocean? She shook her head. "It's too deep."

"I bet it's not," Melinda said. "Come on."

Andi took a big breath for courage and ran after her sister. She stepped into the water. To her surprise and relief, it was only a few inches deep. And just a little colder than the creeks on the Circle C this time of year.

Why, the ocean wasn't scary at all!

A fresh wave slopped against Andi's knees and soaked the edge of her dress. She jumped back. Water splashed her face. "It's salty!"

Andi knew the ocean was salty, but she had never tasted it for herself. It was exciting to make her own discovery.

The girls spent the rest of the afternoon exploring the seashore.

The rocky pools were full of colorful, flower-like creatures with waving tentacles. Others looked like orange or lavender stars. Melinda called them starfish.

Andi giggled. "They look like stars, but they sure don't look like fish."

Small minnows darted back and forth. If Andi held her hand still, they nibbled her fingers. But try as she might, she could not catch a single one.

Later, Andi turned over a rock near the water's edge. A small creature with claws and legs scuttled away. *What in the world?* She squatted down to study it.

The strange animal was no bigger than a quarter. It spit bubbles from its mouth and ran sideways across the sand. When she poked it, two tiny claws waved at her.

Andi caught the creature before it could crawl back under a rock. It tickled her hands and tried to pinch, but its claws were too tiny to hurt her.

She ran to Aunt Rebecca and held out her prize. "What is this?"

"Eek! Shoo!" Her aunt waved Andi's catch away. "Put that horrid little crab back where you found it."

Andi returned the crab but found another, much bigger one under a different rock. She dropped it in her pocket, along with some pretty shells and pebbles she found.

"You will make a fine pet," she told the crab. "I'll mix a little salt in a jar of water so you'll feel right at home." If her new pet needed *cold* water, she could keep it in the icebox.

She smiled at her plan. "Wait till Cory sees you. He won't believe his eyes."

Melinda joined her just then. "Look, Andi." She pointed out over the water. "If you travel from here straight across the ocean for weeks and weeks, you'll finally bump into Japan."

"Really?" Andi had learned about faraway Japan in school. "It's clear on the other side of the world!"

"Yep."

Andi stood still watching the lapping waves. Somewhere on the other side of the world, a little Japanese girl might be standing on her own seashore, looking out over this same water.

It made Andi feel very small. She shivered. "The world is so much bigger than I thought."

"For in six days the Lord made heaven and earth,

the sea, and all that is in them," Melinda whispered from memory. "It's *God* who is so much bigger than I ever imagined," she said.

Andi nodded. *Why did I think the ocean was scary? God is bigger than all of this.*

"I'm glad you're here, little sister," Melinda said. "I've missed you."

"Me too." Andi smiled.

"Girls!"

Andi and Melinda ran back to the driftwood. "Yes, Auntie?"

"Put on your shoes and stockings. The sun is going down, and it's time for supper. We have reservations at the Cliff House."

Was there no end to this day of surprises?

Aunt Rebecca had set aside her bossy ways, at least for this afternoon. Instead of telling Andi to sit still and act like a lady, she'd let her run and play. She didn't even scold Andi for leaving her hat on a log.

Not once had Andi worried about Mitch or Cory or Choo-nook. Not once had she thought about scarlet fever or how much she wanted to find a doctor to help Dr. Weaver.

Had Aunt Rebecca planned it that way?

Andi didn't know, but when she sat down to brush off her feet, she smiled at her aunt.

"Thank you for bringing us to Lands End," she said. "I had a wonderful afternoon."

⊰ CHAPTER 10 ⊱

Surprise Supper Guest

"**I** am glad you enjoyed our outing, Andrea. However . . ." Aunt Rebecca paused. She stood up from the driftwood log and made a *tsk-tsk* sound with her tongue.

Andi stopped yanking on her stockings. They were not cooperating anyway. Her feet and legs were damp and sandy. "What's wrong?"

Aunt Rebecca heaved a big sigh. "It was a mistake to allow you to run *too* wild. Look at you. Your mussed hair. Your wrinkled stockings and sand-spattered dress."

Andi bit her lip. Aunt Rebecca changed moods quicker than a spring shower.

"The sand will brush right off." Andi jumped up and shook out her skirt. "See? Good as new."

Aunt Rebecca smoothed the hair away from Andi's face. She set her hat on her head. "Keep your hat on. That should cover the worst of the tangles."

Another *tsk-tsk*.

Andi glanced at her sister.

Melinda looked neat as a pin—like always. Her long, blond hair was tied neatly back in a big blue bow. No stray curls fell over her eyes. Nobody would ever guess that Melinda had spent the afternoon at the seashore.

Andi sighed and went back to work on her stockings.

"Mind your manners at supper tonight, child," Aunt Rebecca said when Andi was finally ready. "Important people dine at the Cliff House. You must sit still and not speak unless you are spoken to."

Andi's cheeks burned, but not just from too much sun. "Yes, ma'am."

Aunt Rebecca did not remind Melinda about table manners.

"I want you to be on your best behavior." She took Andi's hand. "Come along."

They plodded up the long, steep road from the beach. By the time they reached the top, Andi was too tired to talk. Maybe even too tired to eat. Sitting at the table sounded like a nice rest.

When Aunt Rebecca led them through the wide doors of the Cliff House, Andi blinked. This place

shouted *well-to-do . . . fancy . . . best behavior.* Andi
scooted next to her aunt and tried to look invisible.

"What do you mean, you cannot find my reservation?" Aunt Rebecca glared at the dark-suited man
behind the front desk.

Andi caught her breath. Her aunt sounded furious.

"This is unacceptable, young man." Aunt Rebecca's blue eyes blazed. "I demand that you seat us at
once."

"I apologize, ma'am," the host said, "but I simply
have no—"

"Rebecca!" A smiling older gentleman and a lady
walked up. "What seems to be the trouble?"

When she explained the reservation mix-up, the
gentleman took care of everything. "You must join
my wife and me for supper. I'll have the waiter set
three extra places."

Aunt Rebecca protested, but the man smiled
wider. "I insist."

"Yes, indeed," his wife added.

"In that case, I accept. Thank you." Aunt Rebecca
followed her friends into the dining room. Andi and
Melinda stayed at her heels.

"Who are these lovely young ladies with you,
Rebecca?" the gentleman asked when everything
was arranged and they were seated around the table.

Andi sat up straight and tried to look like a lovely,
well-behaved young lady.

"My nieces from the valley." Aunt Rebecca smiled. "Melinda and Andrea."

"We are delighted to meet you, my dears," the woman said.

Aunt Rebecca turned to the girls. "These are my dear friends, Dr. and Mrs. Wilcox."

"How do you do," Melinda said right away.

Dr. Wilcox! Andi nearly fell out of her chair in surprise. This nice-looking older man was Aunt Rebecca's physician? She opened her mouth to beg the doctor to come to Fresno.

Her aunt's warning look stopped Andi cold. "How do you d-do," she stammered instead.

Dr. Wilcox smiled. "It looks like you have all enjoyed a fine afternoon at the seashore."

"Yes, sir," Melinda answered.

Andi nodded but didn't say a word.

A few minutes later, the waiter arrived to take their orders. Andi and Melinda were not asked what they wanted to eat. Aunt Rebecca ordered for them.

The long wait for their meal came next. Andi's belly rumbled quietly. Maybe she would be able to eat after all.

Melinda listened to the grown-ups talk, but Andi looked out the window. From here the sea lions looked much closer. She watched them swim and climb up on the rocks.

It sure looked like fun!

The smell of something rich and tasty pulled Andi's gaze away from the sea lions. The waiter set a china plate down in front of her. It held a piece of pinkish-orange meat.

"Salmon," Aunt Rebecca said.

Andi took a small bite. *Delicious!* So were the tiny potatoes in cream sauce, the soft roll, and the funny-looking vegetables. Her stomach settled down after the first few bites.

But Andi's thoughts spun faster than ever.

Seeing Dr. Wilcox reminded Andi that her friends back home were still sick. Mitch was still sick. Dr. Weaver probably did not feel well enough yet to care for them.

Andi wanted to talk to Dr. Wilcox, but she didn't dare speak out of turn. Not with Aunt Rebecca's "speak only when spoken to" ringing in her ears. If only—

Something tickled Andi just above her knee. She twitched. Another poke. She jumped.

Melinda jabbed her. "Sit still."

Andi couldn't sit still. Something kept tickling her. She slipped a hand under the napkin in her lap. She felt her pocket. Pebbles couldn't move.

Pebbles didn't move, but crabs did. Her pet seemed in a hurry to escape his pocket prison. *Oh no!*

"What is the trouble, Andrea?" Aunt Rebecca asked. "Is the food not to your liking?"

"It's very good, but I need"—she swallowed—"I need to use the washroom."

Aunt Rebecca's eyebrows rose. Well-mannered children did not ask to use the washroom during a meal.

Andi felt for the crab. Her fingers found only pebbles and shells. She dug around under her napkin. Her elbow banged the table. The dishes rattled.

"Andrea!" Aunt Rebecca scolded. "What has gotten into you?"

Andi slid both hands under her napkin. *Aha! Gotcha.* "May I please use the—*ouch!*"

She yanked her hands out from under the table. A crab the size of a silver dollar hung from her little finger. "Ow! It's pinching me!" She shook her hand.

The crab dropped from Andi's finger and landed upside down in the middle of the table. It flipped itself over. Then it darted sideways across the white tablecloth.

"Good gracious!" Aunt Rebecca's face turned pale.

Melinda shrieked and jumped out of her chair.

A dozen heads turned their way.

The crab crawled faster. It climbed up and over a roll and then onto Melinda's plate. It buried itself in the middle of her creamed potatoes.

A waiter rushed over. "What seems to be the—"

"Take it away!" Aunt Rebecca pointed a shaky finger at Melinda's plate.

Andi buried her face in her hands. A lump caught in her throat. *Don't cry. Don't cry!*

Silence fell.

Andi did not look up. She didn't want to see her aunt's furious face. Andi had disgraced herself worse than climbing a tree.

Quiet laughter broke the silence. Andi peeked between her fingers. Dr. and Mrs. Wilcox were smiling.

Aunt Rebecca was *not* smiling. Neither was Melinda.

"Don't look so sour, Rebecca," the doctor said. "Remember that 'a merry heart doeth good like a medicine.'" He chuckled. "That was pretty funny."

Aunt Rebecca huffed. She clearly did not agree.

"Cliff House guests are used to seeing crab on their plates," Dr. Wilcox said. "Crab is fine eating. They're just not used to seeing one so small and still wiggling." He laughed louder.

Andi lowered her hands. Dr. Wilcox was being kind, but she felt sick. She could not eat another bite of her now-cold meal. Especially not the creamed potatoes.

Nobody else at the table looked like they wanted to finish their supper either.

Dr. Wilcox ordered dessert instead.

"Your aunt often speaks of her family in the valley, Andrea," he said when the iced sherbet arrived.

"I would like to hear about your ranch, and how you are enjoying the city."

Andi suddenly felt much better. At last she had permission to speak! Dr. Wilcox would soon learn all about the ranch—and all about her sick friends.

She rubbed her sore finger. *Thank you, God, for that crab.*

⇥ CHAPTER 11 ⇤

Shakeup

Andi waited for a scolding every day the following week. She deserved one.

Dr. Wilcox had laughed, but throwing a crab in a fancy restaurant was a shocking thing to do. Andi had shamed Aunt Rebecca. She had shamed Melinda. And the doctor and his wife.

"What will Mother say?" Melinda had whispered that evening.

Andi did not look forward to Justin's next visit. Aunt Rebecca would tell him about the crab, and Justin would tell Mother.

But as the days slipped by, no scolding came. Justin did not visit. Aunt Rebecca acted as if she had forgotten all about their Sunday outing.

Did the kind doctor have something to do with it?

Andi hoped so. She liked Dr. Wilcox. He had listened patiently when she told him about Dr. Weaver and the scarlet fever epidemic. He promised to look into the matter and see what he could do to help.

Andi waited and waited, but Aunt Rebecca did not bring up Dr. Wilcox. Andi knew better than to ask. Her aunt did not allow what she called *badgering*.

So all week long Andi practiced patience. It was almost impossible. Sitting still made Andi fidget or fall asleep. Her sewing sampler looked worse and worse.

The housekeeper finally shooed Andi outdoors every day during Aunt Rebecca's afternoon nap.

"Mrs. Jacobs says I'm too much trouble to keep out of mischief," Andi told Brody one afternoon. "She says I make too much noise."

Brody plucked a half-ripe apple from the treetop where he and Andi had climbed. He took aim at a chipmunk but missed. "Playing outdoors beats being stuck in the house with a grumpy tutor any day."

"Or sewing samplers." Andi threw an apple and missed the chipmunk too.

She carefully lowered herself from the tree. As long as Andi kept herself neat and clean, Aunt Rebecca did not ask questions.

Andi was getting very good at climbing trees like a little lady.

When Andi and Brody were not climbing the

apple tree or brushing the horses, they chased Cleo-patra. Sometimes the cat went after birds. Most of the time, though, she headed for the carriage house to hunt mice.

"She's the sneakiest cat ever," Andi said. "Why don't you keep track of her?"

Brody shrugged. "I try to, but Cook lets her out. She doesn't like Cleo rubbing her ankles and begging for scraps."

"Can't you let Cleo stay outside until she wants back in?"

Brody shook his head. "I'm afraid she'll run away or be trampled in the street."

"Oh, that's right. Cleo is a city cat." Andi pointed. "Whoops! There she goes again."

The orange and brown cat padded across the top of the brick wall. She jumped down into the thick shrubbery and disappeared.

Laughing, Andi and Brody went after her.

* *

After a week and a half of practicing patience, Andi could not wait a minute longer. She asked Aunt Rebecca if Dr. Wilcox had decided to go to Fresno.

It was a bad mistake.

"Do not pry into the affairs of your elders," Aunt Rebecca scolded. "Dr. Wilcox has probably forgotten all about it. He has many responsibilities right here in the city."

Andi's heart sank to her toes. She had been so sure the kind doctor would say yes. "Could you at least ask—"

"Andrea, I warned you about badgering me."

Andi looked at her shoes and sighed. "Yes, ma'am."

"Run along outside." Aunt Rebecca rubbed her forehead. "And for goodness' sake, stay clean."

Andi hurried out the back door before Aunt Rebecca changed her mind. Her aunt might get it in her head to make Andi practice the new embroidery stitch Melinda had learned last week.

Loud meowing brought Andi to a stop under the apple tree. She shaded her eyes and looked up.

"Cleo!" Brody's cat had never climbed so high before. "Come down here. Leave those birds alone."

A louder, longer *meow* answered.

Andi ran across the yard and hiked herself to the top of the wall. "Brody!" she called.

Her friend appeared instantly. He slammed the screen door shut, climbed over the wall, and joined her. "Is it Cleo again? I can't find her anywhere inside."

Andi nodded. "She's way up in the tree this time. Higher than ever. It doesn't look like she wants to come down on her own."

Brody let out a big breath. "She never comes down on her own. Do you think she's stuck?"

City cat. "Maybe. She sounds unhappy."

Another yowl.

"I guess we'll have to go up and get her," Brody said.

"Or leave her up there."

"No!"

Andi sent Brody up the tree first. He always climbed first. Andi didn't want him to see the pantalets she wore under her dress.

Higher and higher Brody climbed. Andi followed.

"I got her!" Brody clutched Cleo under one arm. "I can't hold her and climb down at the same time. I'll hand her to you like we always do. Then I'll climb down and you can hand her to me."

Andi usually dropped the cat to the ground after Brody passed her along.

Not today. Cleo and Brody were too high.

Cleo meowed.

I won't worry about my pantalets, Andi told herself. *Rescuing Cleo is more important.* She reached for the cat.

Just then Andi felt a strange rumbling.

Birds shot into the air. The apple tree began to shake as if a giant fist had grabbed its trunk. The other trees were shaking too.

Andi yelped and grabbed a thick branch with both hands.

The windows in Aunt Rebecca's house rattled.

Overhead, Cleo went wild. She growled and hissed and scratched.

Andi's heart pounded. "What's happening?"

Brody shrieked and lost his grip on the cat. An orange and brown blur raced down the tree trunk.

Brody came next, only he wasn't climbing. *Thunk!* He hit the ground.

The shaking stopped.

Andi didn't let go of the branch. She was too scared to move. What if the tree started shaking again? She didn't want to fall like Brody had.

She looked down. Brody lay sprawled on the ground crying.

Brody's sobs brought Andi out of the tree. Branch by branch, she made her way down. She sighed in relief when her feet touched the ground. She squatted beside her friend.

Brody was holding his arm. "It hurts!" he wailed.

"Lie still," Andi said. "I'll get Aunt Rebecca."

Andi tore into the house like a wild thing. She was too frightened to worry about inside voices and ladylike manners. "Aunt Rebecca! Help!"

A white-faced Aunt Rebecca appeared in the kitchen. When she saw Andi she knelt down and pulled her into a tight hug. "Are you all right, my dear? Are you hurt? I was just coming out to look for you."

Andi nodded. "I'm fine, but Brody's hurt." She started crying. "I was so scared. The ground shook and so did the trees."

"Shh, it's over." Aunt Rebecca brushed the hair back from Andi's face. "It was only an earthquake, and a small one at that."

She stood up. Color returned to her cheeks. "Now, stop crying and tell me about Brody. Let's see what we can do for him."

CHAPTER 12

Good-bye,
San Francisco

Aunt Rebecca might be grumpy and demanding, but she knew how to take charge in an emergency. Five minutes after the earthquake ended, Thomas was carrying Brody next door.

Aunt Rebecca led the way.

Andi watched and waited from her aunt's front porch. She sat on the steps and wished Aunt Rebecca would come home. Or Melinda.

She squeezed her eyes shut. Had the earthquake rattled Melinda's school? Was she hurt? Thomas had left a few minutes ago to pick her up.

Andi had seen the broken knick-knacks and dishes inside the house. Something could have fallen on her sister at school. *Please let Melinda be all right,* she prayed.

It felt like hours before Aunt Rebecca walked up the porch steps. "Brody will be fine. The doctor says he broke his wrist." She sighed. "It's a wonder he didn't crack his head open. Goodness! Falling out of a *tree*."

She looked too tired to scold Andi. "Brody is terribly upset. He's worried about his cat. Do you think you could look for his pet?"

Andi jumped up. Finally! Something she could do to help. "Oh, yes! I know all of Cleo's hiding places."

Aunt Rebecca smiled. "Good. When you find the cat, take her next door. I'll let Mrs. Stanton know."

"Yes, ma'am!" Andi raced around the side of the house and into the back yard. She peered up into the apple tree, but Cleo was not there.

That left the carriage house. Andi pushed through the doors and headed straight for the shelves along the back wall. "Here, Cleo," she called softly.

No answer.

Andi searched high and low. She found the cat lurking under a low shelf. "Come on."

Cleo did not come willingly. She hissed and growled, but Andi did not let go. Cleo ripped into Andi until bright-red scratches covered her arms and hands.

"Ouch!" Andi dragged her out. "You ungrateful cat."

Injured and filthy, Andi held Cleo tightly against her chest and ran out of the carriage house. She clattered up the back steps and cut through the house. A minute later she was standing on Brody's front porch.

She rang the bell.

"You found Master Brody's cat!" The housekeeper smiled and showed Andi into the parlor.

Brody rested on his mother's best sofa. His wrist was wrapped up tight and he wore a sling. When he saw Andi and Cleo, he cried out his joy. "Thank you, Andi!"

Cleo curled up beside Brody and began to purr.

"Andrea Carter, just look at you." Aunt Rebecca shook her head. "You are a sight."

Andi didn't answer. She was staring at the doctor.

He sat next to Brody and stroked the cat. "Cleo, you are more trouble than you're worth sometimes."

"Dr. Wilcox?" Andi whispered.

He chuckled. "Hello, Andrea. It's nice to see you again. Thank you for finding Brody's cat. He's especially fond of Cleopatra."

There were dozens—maybe hundreds—of doctors in San Francisco. The surprise at seeing Aunt Rebecca's doctor tending Brody made her stammer, "W-what are you doing here?"

"This young scamp needed a doctor to bind up his wrist." Dr. Wilcox ruffled Brody's hair. "Leave it to you to be up in a tree when an earthquake hits. More gray hair for your poor mother."

"But, Grandfather!" Brody pouted. "We had to get Cleo down. We just had to."

Grandfather? Andi's eyes widened. "You're Brody's grandfather?"

"I am. I'm also your aunt's good friend and physician." Dr. Wilcox reached out and took Andi's hands. "I've thought about our talk over supper last Sunday evening."

"Will you come?" Andi asked.

Dr. Wilcox nodded. "I'm taking the train tomorrow to see what kind of damage the scarlet fever epidemic is doing. I also convinced another physician to join me. There may be more than one worn-out doctor in the valley."

"Oh, thank you!" Andi threw her arms around his neck. "Thank you."

"Now, let me take care of those ugly scratches on your hands," the doctor said. "They must sting like crazy."

A few minutes later the Stantons' housekeeper brought in a tray of tea and cookies. She also brought Melinda, who looked pale but unharmed.

"Hi, Melinda," Brody greeted her. "Sit down. It's a party."

Mrs. Stanton didn't seem to mind that her son was grass-stained and rumpled. Aunt Rebecca didn't seem to mind that dirt covered Andi's dress. Or that her hair was tangled and mussed.

What a surprising afternoon!

Brody helped himself to three cookies. He gave Cleo a bite.

Dr. Wilcox settled himself into a large easy chair and sipped his tea. "Was this your first earthquake, girls?"

"Yes, sir," Melinda said. "It was frightening, but nobody at school got hurt."

Andi stopped chewing. She remembered the shaking tree. Brody's crying. The frantic cat and the flying birds. She shivered. "Yes, sir."

"Stick around this part of the country, and you'll no doubt experience many more," Dr. Wilcox said. "This one was just a hiccup. I remember the big quake back in '68." He whistled. "Wasn't that a dandy?"

The grown-ups spent the next half hour telling earthquake stories.

Andi listened, spellbound. Their stories made today's earthquake sound not as scary.

Now I have an earthquake story to tell too, she thought. *So does Melinda. Wait till Mother hears!*

The housekeeper came in and announced a visitor. "Mr. Carter, ma'am."

"Howdy," Mitch greeted them. "Mrs. Jacobs said you were all over here."

"Stars above, Mitchell," Aunt Rebecca burst out. "What are you doing in the city?"

"Mitch!" Andi and Melinda yelled.

"You're well!" Andi leaped from her chair and raced across the parlor. Melinda was one step behind her.

Mitch wrapped his arms around his sisters and hugged them. "It's good to see you. The quake gave me a little scare. Thankfully, it didn't last long enough to *really* worry me."

"Do you know how Sarah is?" Melinda asked.

"What about Cory? And Choo-nook?" Andi added.

Mitch laughed. "One at a time, please." He sat down on a small sofa.

Andi plopped down beside him. Mrs. Stanton fixed him a steaming cup of tea.

"The fever has burned itself out," Mitch said. "There are no new cases in town or on the ranch. Mother thought Andi might want to come home for her birthday." He winked. "It's this Sunday, you know."

Andi bounced up and down, nearly upsetting her brother's teacup.

"Hey, be careful." Mitch lifted his cup out of the way. "Chad won't put me back to work yet, so Mother sent me to surprise you."

Andi didn't think her heart could hold so many surprises.

"And our friends?" Melinda asked.

"Your friends have recovered, as far as I know," Mitch said.

Then he looked down at Andi with a sad sort of smile.

Andi held her breath.

"Choo-nook is fine now, although her little brother did not make it."

Tears welled up in Andi's eyes.

Mitch pulled her into a hug. "Four children in town died as well, all under the age of six. The others are recovering but are not completely out of danger. Dr. Weaver is barely managing."

"He won't have to manage alone for long." Dr. Wilcox stood and introduced himself. "My physician friends and I will bring fresh medicine and cheerful smiles. What more do recovering patients need?"

Andi rubbed away her tears. "When can we leave, Mitch?"

"First thing tomorrow morning."

"Why don't you stay a few days, Mitchell," Aunt Rebecca suggested. "We could give Andrea quite a party. I know all the right people."

Andi scooted closer to Mitch. She did not want to stay in the city one day longer than she had to. Too bad Melinda had to stay until the end of the school term.

Mitch gave Andi's hand a don't-worry squeeze. "I'm sorry, Aunt Rebecca, but Mother is expecting us."

Andi put her arms around her brother's neck. "Thank you, Aunt Rebecca, but my best birthday is having Mitch well and going home to the ranch."

She could almost hear the train wheels clacking their noisy song: Going home! Going home!

Good-bye, San Francisco. I'm going home!

History Fun
Scarlet Fever

Scarlet fever is a children's disease, but people of any age can catch it. It's highly contagious. The bacteria infect the throat, making it very sore and painful to swallow. There is usually a high fever, body aches, chills, and a headache.

A few days later, the fever goes down and a reddish rash breaks out. It looks like goosebumps on a sunburn. The rash starts out on the child's neck and face then spreads to the rest of the body. About a week later it begins to fade. Patients often have a "strawberry tongue"—red, swollen, and bumpy.

Scarlet fever is the same infection that causes

strep throat. However, the rash hardly ever appears in these modern times. Antibiotics kill the bacteria before they can do much harm. Even without medicine, this disease is not as dangerous today as it was during Andi's time.

Throughout history, scarlet fever was considered a mild childhood illness. Then it suddenly changed for the worse. No one knows why, but in the mid 1800s scarlet fever began to break out in deadly epidemics across Europe and America.

Hearing that the disease was in the area sent fear into every mother's heart, just like it did for Andi's mother. Scarlet fever was a killer of children in those days. Sick grown-ups might feel miserable, but they rarely died. They never got the rash either.

No one knew how scarlet fever spread or whom it might infect. There was no medicine to cure it. A family sometimes lost half their children in a week or two. A few years later, scarlet fever would return to strike again.

The children who lived sometimes suffered from the infection's damage. For example, many believe Helen Keller became blind and deaf from scarlet fever in 1882 when she was not even two years old.

Then around 1885, scarlet fever suddenly changed back to a milder disease, at least in modernized countries. It has stayed that way right up to the present. Hardly anyone catches scarlet fever today.

**For more Andi fun,
download free activity pages
at CircleCSteppingStones.com.**

Susan K. Marlow is always on the lookout for a new story, whether she's writing books, teaching writing workshops, or sharing what she's learned as a homeschooling mom. Susan is the author of several series set in the Old West—ranging from new reader to young adult—and she enjoys relaxing on her fourteen-acre homestead in the great state of Washington. Connect with the author at CircleCSteppingStones.com or by emailing Susan at SusanKMarlow@kregel.com.

Leslie Gammelgaard, illustrator of the Circle C Beginnings and Circle C Stepping Stones series, lives in beautiful Washington state where every season delights the senses. Along with illustrating books, Leslie inspires little people (especially her four grandchildren) to explore and express their creative nature through art and writing.

Grow Up with Andi!

Don't miss any of Andi's adventures in the Circle C Beginnings series

Andi's Pony Trouble
Andi's Indian Summer
Andi's Fair Surprise
Andi's Scary School Days
Andi's Lonely Little Foal
Andi's Circle C Christmas

For readers ages 9–13!

**Andi's adventures continue in
the Circle C Adventures series**

Andrea Carter and the Long Ride Home
Andrea Carter and the Dangerous Decision
Andrea Carter and the Family Secret
Andrea Carter and the San Francisco Smugglers
Andrea Carter and the Trouble with Treasure
Andrea Carter and the Price of Truth

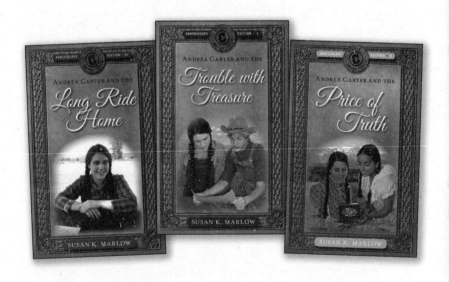

**Free enrichment activities are available at
CircleCAdventures.com.**